Jen
the
Hen

Colin and
Jacqui Hawkins

DORLING KINDERSLEY
London • New York • Stuttgart

Have you heard of Jen the hen?

h

One day she went to her den.

Jen looked in her bag for paper and pen.

Then she wrote a letter to Ken and Ben, the garden men.

m

Jen signed it and stamped it,
and gave it to Wren.

Wren flew over the glen
looking for Ken and Ben.

B

Ken and Ben
The Garden Men

She landed on Ben and gave the letter to Ken.

The letter from Jen said to meet her at ten.

Exactly at ten, they all met in the glen – Wren, Ken, Ben, and a hen called Jen.

A DORLING KINDERSLEY BOOK

Published in the United Kingdom in 1995
by Dorling Kindersley Limited,
9 Henrietta Street, London WC2E 8PS

Published in the United States in 1995
by Dorling Kindersley Publishing, Inc.,
95 Madison Avenue, New York, New York 10016

2 4 6 8 10 9 7 5 3

ISBN 0-7513-5350-7 (UK)
ISBN 0-7894-0175-4 (US)

Reproduction by DOT Gradations
Printed in Italy by L.E.G.O.